THE LIFE SCIENCE LIBRARY™

Plant Development
and Growth

Isaac Nadeau

The Rosen Publishing Group's
PowerKids Press™
New York

To Becca

Published in 2006 by The Rosen Publishing Group, Inc.
29 East 21st Street, New York, NY 10010

First Edition

Editor: Rachel O'Connor
Book Design: Albert Hanner

Photo Credits: Cover, pp. 1, 17 © Robert Essel NYC/Corbis; p. 5 (top) © Walter Hodges/Corbis; p.5 (middle) © Clouds Hill Imaging Ltd./Corbis; p. 5 (bottom) © Royalty-Free/Corbis; p. 6 © Ron Boardman, Frank Lane Picture Agency/Corbis; p. 7 (top) © Anthony Banister, Gallo Images/Corbis; p. 9 © Davies & Starr/Getty Images; p. 11 (top) © Paul A. Souders/Corbis; p. 11 (middle and detail) © David Aubrey/Corbis; p. 13 by Michelle Innes; p. 14 © Keren Su/Corbis; p. 15 (top) © Tania Midgley/Corbis; p. 15 (bottom) © Jim Zuckerman/Corbis; p. 16 © Hal Horwitz/Corbis; p. 19 © Ron Sanford/Corbis; p. 21 (top) © Martin B. Withers, Frank Lane Picture Agency/Corbis; p. 21 (bottom) © Chinch Gryniewicz; Ecoscene/Corbis.

Library of Congress Cataloging-in-Publication Data

Nadeau, Isaac.
Plant development and growth / Isaac Nadeau.— 1st ed.
p. cm. — (The life science library)
Includes index.
ISBN 1-4042-2820-9 (library binding)
1. Growth (Plants)—Juvenile literature. 2. Plants—Development—Juvenile literature. I. Title. II. Life science library (New York, N.Y.)

QK731.N33 2005
571.8'2—dc22
2005001749

Manufactured in the United States of America

Contents

What Makes a Plant a Plant?

There are thousands of different kinds of plants. They come in a wide range of sizes, shapes, and colors, but they all have a few things in common. Each plant is made up of cells. Plant cells have tough walls, which help plants stand up straight without **skeletons**. Most plants have leaves, which sprout from the ends of stems and branches, and roots that hold them into the ground. Leaves and roots help plants get the **energy** and **nutrients** they need to live and grow.

Many types of plants, such as tulips and roses, have flowers. Some types of plants also have fruits, such as apple trees or vines that produce grapes. Other plants, like pine trees and ferns, do not have flowers or fruits.

One of the most important parts of a plant is the leaf. This is because the leaf is in charge of photosynthesis, which is the way in which the plant gets its food, or energy. The leaf is also in charge of respiration, or breathing.

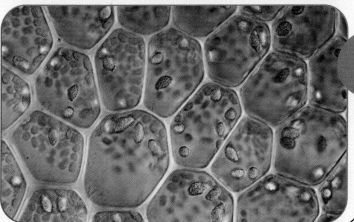

Here is a close-up photograph of plant cells. The weblike shapes are the cell walls, which help protect the cell.

This diagram shows the main parts of a plant. Each part of the plant has a different job. For example, the roots take in water and nutrients from the soil and bring them to the rest of the plant. The stem helps bring the nutrients up to the flower part of the plant. The flower plays an important role in helping the plant to reproduce, or create new plants.

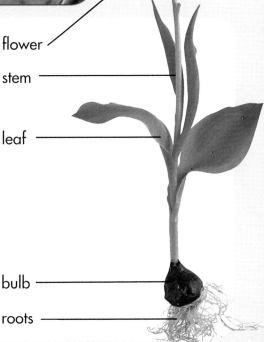

flower

stem

leaf

bulb

roots

How Plants Begin

Most plants start as seeds. In flowering plants seeds are formed when **pollen** from the male part of a plant, called the anther, travels to the stigma, which is the sticky tip of the female part. The female part is called the pistil. As the pollen makes its way down the pistil, it touches the egg, which is inside the **ovary.** When this happens the egg is **fertilized**. The egg begins to grow into a seed inside the flower. Seeds can be smaller than a grain of sand. The biggest seed is a coconut. A seed has an outer coat, which helps guard it from the weather. Seeds are packed with the nutrients that the young plant inside the seed needs to grow.

Pollination occurs when pollen is moved from the anther to the stigma. When this happens in just one plant, it is called self-pollination. When it happens between two plants, it is called cross-pollination. Bees like the one pictured to the left help in cross-pollination by carrying pollen from plant to plant.

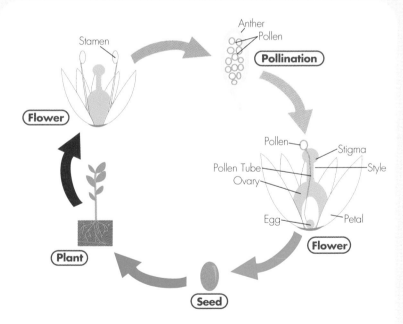

Stamen

Anther
Pollen
Pollination

Flower

Pollen
Stigma
Pollen Tube
Style
Ovary
Egg
Petal
Flower

Plant

Seed

This diagram shows all the stages in the growth of a plant. After pollination a seed is formed. The seed then grows into a plant. As the plant gets older, it produces flowers and sometimes fruits as well.

Sprouting Seeds

Most seeds never grow into plants. Many are eaten by animals. Others are unable to reach the kind of soil in which they need to grow. Plants produce a lot of seeds to increase the chance that a few seeds may germinate, or sprout.

From the very beginning, water is important to the life of a plant. A seed begins to grow when water from the soil softens the seed and makes its way inside its outer coat. A single root is the first part of the young plant to grow from the seed. The root goes down into the soil. Next a small shoot begins to grow up through the soil. When this shoot reaches the surface, the plant's first leaves unfold toward the sunlight.

Here you can see the early stages of the growth of a sunflower seed. The growth of a seed into a plant is called germination. The seed has everything a plant needs to grow. At the beginning of germination, which is shown here, a part of the seed called a radicle breaks through the seed. The radicle grows into the plant's roots. The next stages in germination follow when the stem and leaves push their way through the seed.

Hungry Roots

Many plants have more of their bodies under the ground than above it. This is where the plant's roots are found. Roots grow downward and help secure the plant into the ground. Another important job of roots is to take in water and nutrients from the soil. This helps in the growth of the plant. Soil is considered **fertile** if it is filled with **elements** such as nitrogen, potassium, and phosphorous, which are necessary for plants to grow. These elements must be mixed with the water in the soil for the roots to **absorb** them. Once this mixture is absorbed by the roots, it travels to the leaves where it is changed into food that the plant can use.

When we eat carrots, we are eating the root part of the plant. Carrots are a great source of vitamin A, which is good for healthy hair, teeth, and skin. However, if you eat too many carrots your skin can turn orange! Don't worry, even if this happens, it is not harmful.

The root of a plant contains different parts. There is the primary root, which is the main root. There are the secondary roots, which are not as big as the primary root and grow sideways. The root hairs cover the roots. They absorb the nutrients from the soil. In the close-up picture, you can see the tiny root hairs sprouting from the root.

Photosynthesis

All living things, from grasses to gorillas, need energy to exist. Without energy no living thing would be able to move or grow, including plants. Plants are called producers because they are able to create energy from sunlight. This is called photosynthesis. The job of the leaves on a plant is to collect sunlight. The leaves also collect a gas from the air called carbon dioxide. The mixture of water and nutrients is pumped, or pushed, up from the roots to the leaves. Inside the leaf the carbon dioxide, water, and nutrients are combined. When sunlight hits the leaf, a **chemical reaction** occurs that turns this mix into sugar. Plants use this sugar to gain energy and grow.

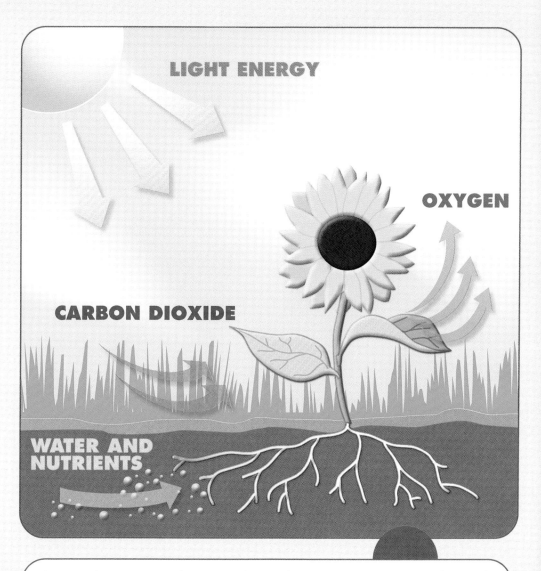

LIGHT ENERGY

OXYGEN

CARBON DIOXIDE

WATER AND NUTRIENTS

Photosynthesis comes from Greek words meaning "to put together with light." Photosynthesis is the way in which a plant makes food for itself. It mostly takes place in the leaves of the plant. The leaves hold green matter called chlorophyll, which absorbs the energy that comes from the Sun. The chlorophyll helps bring about the chemical reaction that changes carbon dioxide, water, and nutrients into sugar, or food for the plant.

Staying Alive

There are many conditions that plants need to be healthy. In addition to sunlight, plants need enough space in the soil for their roots to grow to get enough food. If too many plants are crowded together, there may not be enough food for all of them. Plants can also get too much water. When this happens a plant's roots may have a hard time breathing, and the plant could die. Even if all the conditions for growth are met, the plant can always be eaten by a hungry animal or be stepped on by a person's foot. Whenever you see a full-grown plant, you are looking at a living thing that has been able to **survive** against the odds.

Plants need enough sunlight to photosynthesize. This is why many plants cannot grow in the shade.

Plants, such as the tree shown here, can die when it is too hot and there is not enough water. Only certain plants, like cacti, can survive the hot weather in desert areas. Plants can also die when it is too cold.

Reaching for the Sun

In some cases, as with some plants that live on treeless plains, there is a danger of them getting too much light. Plants such as the yellow compass plant, shown here, are able to turn their leaves away from the Sun if they are getting too much sunlight.

Some people believe the sunflower got its name because the flower head on a sunflower looks like the Sun. There is another reason. If you watch a sunflower on a sunny day, you will notice that the flower head turns slowly throughout the day so that it is always facing the Sun. Look closely at plants in your home or in your classroom. You will notice that most of their leaves are turned toward the window, where the sunlight comes in. Plants have a special ability to reach their leaves toward the Sun to get as much sunlight as they need. This is called heliotropism.

The scientific name for sunflower is Helianthus. "Helios" is the Greek word meaning "Sun" and "anthus" means "flower." The larger types of sunflowers usually grow to between 6 and 10 feet (2–3 m) tall. The smaller types can grow to between 1 and 2 feet (.3–.6 m) tall.

Flowers and Fruits

There are more than 250,000 kinds of flowering plants in the world. Flowers, such as the Arctic poppy, can be found in the cold Arctic. Others, such as orchids, are found on **tropical** islands. There are flowers on mountaintops and in dry deserts. Many flowers, such as roses, have sweet smells. Smells help **attract** bees, butterflies, and other insects that can help pollinate the flower. Flowers come in many different colors that also help attract bees and other insects.

When some plants become pollinated, a fruit, such as an apple or orange, begins to grow inside them. The plant's flowers are no longer needed to attract insects. Fruits are the next stage in a plant's seasonal growth.

Many fruits are colorful and tasty so they attract birds and other animals. When birds eat these fruits and fly away, they carry the seeds in their stomachs. When the birds get rid of the food, the seeds are planted far away and can grow into new plants.

19

Starting Again

Over time plants have found ways to move their seeds from one place to another. Plants cannot walk. Instead wind, water, animals, and **gravity** help carry and plant their seeds for them. For example dandelion seeds are light and fluffy, so the wind can carry the seeds great distances. Burrs, which come from the burdock plant, are able to stick to the fur of an animal as it passes. After the animal has walked some distance, seeds fall out of the burr and plant themselves. Coconuts can float for miles (km) in ocean waters until they are washed up on shore and can begin to grow. These are just a few examples of the ways in which seeds move from place to place.

The helicopter shape of a maple seed helps the wind carry it a short distance from the parent plant, where it has room to grow.

Not many people know that dandelions can be eaten, and they are full of healthful nutrients! They are weeds, however, and gardeners everywhere try very hard to get rid of them. This is not easy to do, since the dandelion seeds are spread very easily because they are so light and fluffy.

Grow Plants at Home

You can learn a lot about plants by growing one yourself at home. There are many kinds of plants you can grow. First you will need a pot and some soil. Plant your seeds in the soil, usually no more than 1 inch (2.5 cm) deep. You may want to place two seeds in a pot, in case one of them does not germinate. Place the pot close to a sunny window. You should water your plant about twice a week. Check on it every day. In about one week you should see the first shoots begin to sprout.

In the summer, when the weather is warmer, you could try growing plants outside. You might try growing carrots or tomatoes. There is nothing better than tasting a plant that you helped grow!

Glossary

absorb (ub-ZORB) To take in and hold on to something.

attract (uh-TRAKT) To cause people, animals, or things to want to be near you.

chemical reaction (KEH-mih-kul ree-AK-shun) What happens when matter is mixed with other matter to cause changes.

elements (EH-lih-ments) The basic matter of which all things are made.

energy (EH-nur-jee) The power to work or to act.

fertile (FER-tul) Good for making and growing things.

fertilized (FUR-tuh-lyzd) Put male cells inside an egg to make babies.

gravity (GRA-vih-tee) The natural force that causes objects to move toward the center of Earth.

nutrients (NOO-tree-ints) Food that a living thing needs to live and to grow.

ovary (OH-vuh-ree) The part of a flowering plant in which seeds are formed.

pollen (PAH-lin) A powder made by the male parts of flowers.

skeletons (SKEH-lih-tunz) The bones in animals' or people's bodies.

survive (sur-VYV) To stay alive.

tropical (TRAH-puh-kul) Having to do with the warm parts of Earth that are near the equator.

Index

Web Sites

Due to the changing nature of Internet links, PowerKids Press has developed an online list of Web sites related to the subject of this book. This site is updated regularly. Please use this link to access the list:
www.powerkidslinks.com/lsl/devlplant/